THE INVISIBLE SPY

Mark Fowler

Designed and illustrated by
Peter Wingham

Edited by
Phil Roxbee Cox

Contents

About this book

The Invisible Spy plunges you into the world of secret formulas, kidnap, spies and counter-spies. Throughout the book there are lots of tricky puzzles which you must solve in order to understand the next part of the story. If you get stuck there are clues on page 43 and you can check the answers on pages 44 to 48.

Series Editor: Gaby Waters
Assistant Series Editor: Michelle Bates

The Urgent Message

Lucy Lambert, junior reporter at the Hardfax News Agency, was late.

She gulped. She should have been back from lunch hours ago.

Panting, she reached the office, punched her number into the electronic lock . . .

. . . and rushed inside, only to stop dead in her tracks. The room was in chaos. Papers were strewn everywhere and drawers gaped open.

Worst of all, the whole place was deserted. Where was everyone? What had happened? Suddenly the special Hardfax Hotline began to ring. Lucy lifted the receiver.

Instantly a voice started blurting out complicated instructions. Without giving Lucy a chance to reply, the mysterious caller abruptly hung up.

Just then, Lucy spotted a note pinned to a board. As she read, her heart sank.

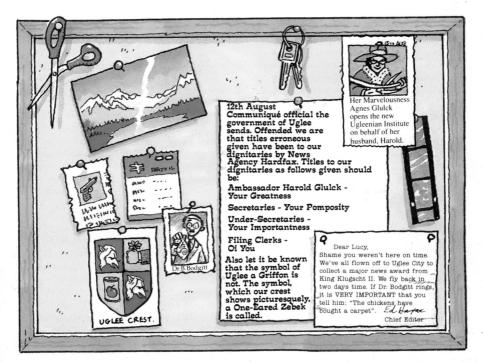

She should have given a vital message to Dr. Bodgitt. There was only one thing to do. She'd have to go to the meeting point and deliver the message in person.

She knew how to find Trankwill Square, but what were the greetings that she would need?

Do you know?

3

Smokescreen

This was a case for the Hardfax emergency transport. Lucy checked the bell, then set off at full speed.

When she reached Trankwill Square, a scene of utter pandemonium greeted her. Dense clouds of smoke billowed everywhere, and people rushed about in panic, coughing and spluttering.

What was going on? Lucy began to listen to the people talking. It all seemed very strange.

At that moment, a clock struck four. As the smoke began to clear, Lucy spotted the meeting point.

Where is it?

. . . a funny popping noise, a loud WHOOSH! and suddenly the square was filled with smoke . . . no one knows where it's all coming from.

. . . not a stone's throw from the Pyrites Institute, one of the most important scientific laboratories in the country.

. . . security expert Babs McGinty is on the scene, explaining about the cameras and sensors she installed inside the institute.

Strangers Meet

Lucy hurried over to the archway.

"Your Marvelousness . . . ?" she called into the darkness, feeling rather silly.

"Your Greatness," replied a figure, stepping forward.

"But you're not Dr. Bodgitt," said Lucy, staring at the new arrival.

"And you're not a chief editor," replied the figure. "You're too young. How do you know the right codewords?"

"How do you know that I know the right codewords?" asked Lucy, feeling bewildered. "And what are you doing here anyway?"

There was a moment's silence, then the stranger began to explain.

My name's Jack. I sometimes work as a junior under-assistant to Dr. Bodgitt. I - er - clean up when he has finished his experiments.

This afternoon he asked me to deliver an urgent message to Mr. Hardfax. He told me where to go, and explained about the codewords.

Moments later I heard a commotion in his laboratory. I went inside and found that the window was open and Dr. Bodgitt had vanished.

Lucy gasped. What could they do now? Dr. Bodgitt had disappeared and Ed Hardfax was on his way to Uglee City.

"We'll have to read the message," said Jack, tearing open the envelope. "It might give us a clue."

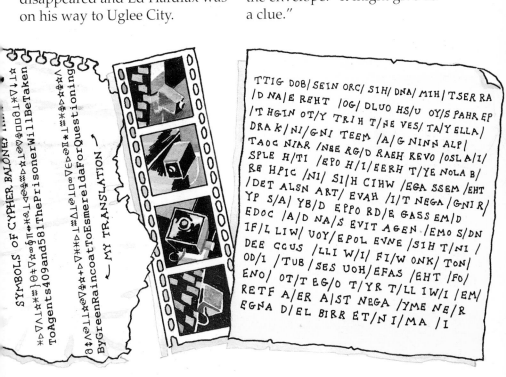

SYMBOLS OF CYPHER BALONEY !!!!

✦▽∨⅄l✦☆∗⌐]⊕∀▽☆∞⊕Π∗∗⊙∟∗◇θ⌐⊕ψ◇∅□□⌐l☆∨⅃l✦
*✦▽⅄l☆☆∗⌐]⊕∀▽☆∞⊕Π∗∗⊙ l◁⊄⅄∆▽⅄l⊕∨♀∅□□⌐l☆∨⅃l✦ ToAgents409and581ThePrisonerWillBeTaken

θ♯∀θ⅃l☆⅄⊕∨θ☆∗∆▽∀∨∗∗⊙ l⊕⊙□l◁∆∆∨θ☆◁∨l∗∗⊙▽◇∨∆✦⅄♯ ByGreenRaincoatToEsmereldaForQuestioning
⌐ MY TRANSLATION ⌐

TTIG DOB/ SEIN ORC/ S1H/ DNA/ MIH/ TSER RA
/D NA/E REHT /OG/ DLUO HS/U OY/S PAHR EP
/T HGIN OT/Y TRIH T/NE VES/ TA/Y ELLA/
DRA K/ NI/ GNI TEEM /A/G NINN ALP/
TAOC NIAR /NEE RG/D RAEH REVO /OSL A/I/
SPLE H/TI /EPO H/I/ EERH T/YE NOLA B/
RE HPIC /NI/ SIH CIHW /EGA SSEM /EHT
/DET ALSN ART/ EVAH /I/T NEGA /GNI R/
YP S/A/ YB/D EPPO RD/E GASS EM/D
EDOC /A/D NA/S EVIT AGEN /EMO S/DN
IF/L LIW/ UOY/ EPOL EVNE /SIH T/NI /
DEE CCUS /LLI W/I/ FI/W ONK/ TON/
OD/I /TUB /SES UOH/ EFAS /EHT /FO/
ENO/ OT/T EG/O T/YR T/LL IW/I /EM/
RETF A/ER A/ST NEGA /YME NE/R
EGNA D/EL BIRR ET/N I/MA /I

Inside they found a strip of negatives, together with a scrap of torn paper and a strange looking letter.

"It must be in code," said Lucy, trying to understand the writing.

What does the letter say?

Down Dark Alleys

Enemy agents? Safe house? Green Raincoat? What did it all mean? And how come Ed Hardfax had the power to arrest people? There was only one hope of finding out what was going on.

"Let's go to Kard Alley and see what happens at the meeting," said Jack, as they hurried to the nearest metro station. "We have exactly half an hour."

Soon they arrived at East Docks Station. Lucy and Jack climbed up to street level.

"I know the way from here," said Lucy, setting off along a deserted passageway. "I was in the alley last week reporting on the case of the stolen lobster pots."

Ten minutes later, she wasn't feeling quite so certain of the route. It was getting dark as they crept closer to the docks. A strange fishy smell hung in the air while seagulls screeched overhead.

A streetlamp clicked on as they scurried along a dark passageway. Lucy was beginning to wonder if they'd taken a wrong turn.

Then at last they rounded a corner and found themselves in Kard Alley. Jack checked his watch. It was 7:30 exactly.

At that moment, a man in a raincoat emerged from the shadows. At the other end of the alley, a second man appeared.

As the two men passed, the one in the raincoat handed over an envelope, muttering something about "proof" and "kidnap".

The other man opened the envelope, and glanced at the contents. He tore them up, tossing the pieces to the ground.

As soon as the coast was clear, Lucy and Jack rushed forward and picked up the torn scraps.

"It's a photo," said Jack. "I wonder why it's so important?"

"If we can fit the pieces together, perhaps it'll help us to understand what's going on," said Lucy, getting to work.

What does the photo show?

9

Message in the Attic

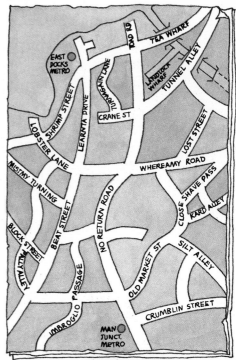

Lucy and Jack looked at each other aghast.

"Dr. Bodgitt has been kidnapped!" exclaimed Jack.

They had to help him. But where should they start?

"At least we know where he's been taken," Jack said, pointing to a road name shown in the photo. "Block Street. But where's that?"

"We'll soon find out," said Lucy, foraging in her pockets. "Hardfax reporters always carry a map."

Lucy and Jack plunged back into the maze of deserted streets.

They reached Block Street, and frantically searched for Number 12, the building in the photo. At last they found it.

Cautiously, Lucy and Jack crept inside.

"This way," hissed Lucy, leading the way up a flight of stairs.

They tiptoed through an empty room, then found themselves at the foot of a ladder. Hesitantly, they began to climb.

They emerged into an attic room, filled with junk. There was no sign of Dr. Bodgitt, but someone had obviously been there recently.

Searching the room, Lucy found a clipping from a newspaper.

A ring had been drawn around a strangely worded ad. In a flash of inspiration, Lucy realized that it contained a hidden message.

What does the message say?

Jetty by Moonlight

ESMERELDA

The moon glinted on the water as, half an hour later, Jack and Lucy reached jetty number twenty.

"The newspaper message told the kidnappers to bring Dr. Bodgitt here," said Lucy. "But where is he now?"

"He must be on board one of the boats," said Jack. "We've just got to find out which."

Lucy suddenly remembered the scrap of paper from Dr. Bodgitt's envelope. She was sure it held a vital clue.

Which boat are the kidnappers using?

THE POLLY ANNA
2

SEA 1st

THE ALBERTA

Countdown to Chaos

Our guest is with the octopus in the boiler room.

Silently, Lucy and Jack crept closer to the rusting hulk of the *Esmerelda*.

"There's a ladder over there," whispered Lucy excitedly, pointing to the stern of the ship. "Follow me!"

Just as they had climbed onto the deck, they heard footsteps.

"Hide!" hissed Jack, diving for cover.

With pounding hearts, they slipped through a doorway, and climbed down a steep ladder. The only sound was the lapping of water against the ship. At one point Lucy heard a noise, but it was just someone snoring.

At last they stood outside the boiler room. There was no sign of Dr. Bodgitt, but there were two burly guards playing cards. Jack was sure the scientist was inside one of the packing crates, but how could they release him?

Crouching behind a packing case, Jack and Lucy watched as two sinister figures appeared on the deck, talking in low voices.

Lucy was convinced that the men were talking about Dr. Bodgitt. She and Jack had to find the boiler room. They were in luck. Creeping along the deck, they spotted a plan of the ship with the boiler room marked on it!

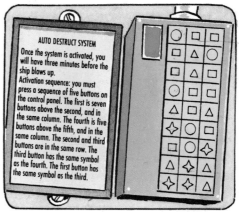

At that moment, Lucy caught sight of a strange looking keypad. Next to it was a notice headed: "Auto Destruct System".

A desperate plan began to form in Lucy's mind.

"If we can activate the auto destruct, the guards will be forced to abandon ship," she whispered. "That will give us the chance to rescue Dr. Bodgitt."

What is the activation sequence?

Dr. Bodgitt – Special Agent

This ship will self destruct in exactly three minutes.

As Lucy punched the last button, a recorded message blared out. In moments the ship was thrown into turmoil.

The guards in the boiler room leaped up in panic, racing to the ladders. Sirens wailed as the crew of the *Esmerelda* dashed to safety.

You have twenty seconds, nineteen, eighteen . . .

BOOM!

Lucy and Jack rushed over to the crate marked *Octopus*, and pulled out, among other things, a dazed Dr. Bodgitt.

Before he fully realized what was happening, the doctor was being helped off the side of the ship. Time was running out!

Still confused, he found himself running for his life. When they finally reached safety, he told them his strange story . . .

As you no doubt know, I am a scientist and inventor with an international reputation. What you will not know however is that I lead a double life . . .

. . . twenty years ago I was recruited as an agent for a secret organization. We are committed to making sure that science is only used to help people, not to harm them.

Recently I was posted to the Pyrites Institute where scientists have discovered a powerful new substance called Xyl-o-phone 280. And I mean powerful.

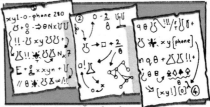

Xyl-o-phone 280 is capable of generating huge amounts of heat and power without creating radiation. In the wrong hands, however, a single grain could destroy a city.

Somehow, agents of a dangerous organization called The World Leaders of Tomorrow have infiltrated the Institute. They have captured three quarters of the Xyl-o-phone formula.

To do this, they have eluded the most advanced security equipment in the world. There is even a special camera inside the vault where the formula is hidden . . .

. . . but the enemy spy hasn't shown up on a single video recording. That is why we call this agent of evil "The Invisible Spy". No one even knows what he – or she – looks like.

Then today I discovered that the World Leaders of Tomorrow had hired a local gang led by "Green Raincoat" to kidnap me. Despite a carefully planned escape, I fell into their clutches.

Back at the Lab

The envelope contains a message in a code known as Fiendish Fish One. This is only used for highly important communications.

An invisible spy? Lucy and Jack stared at Dr. Bodgitt aghast. Then suddenly Lucy remembered something.

"One of the guards dropped this as he made his escape," she said, holding out a sealed envelope.

Dr. Bodgitt ripped open the envelope, then his eyes lit up. "Follow me!" he cried, diving into the nearest metro station. Lucy and Jack struggled to keep up.

Soon they were back on the street and nearing a dusty store crammed full of old cameras.

"I have a secret laboratory in the basement," explained Dr. Bodgitt. "I've been developing a machine to crack Fiendish Fish One. We must hurry."

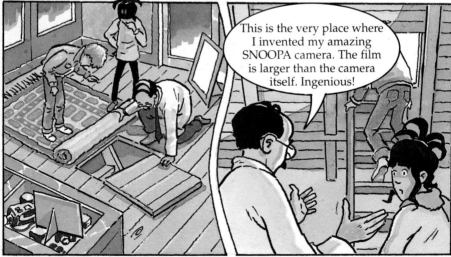

This is the very place where I invented my amazing SNOOPA camera. The film is larger than the camera itself. Ingenious!

The Chase is on

There was only one thing to do. They'd have to go to Umbrella Alley and follow Agent Ambel as he set out on his mission. Out of nowhere Dr. Bodgitt produced devices like toy telephones.

"We'll keep in touch using these Megatuff Radios," he said.

As they slipped into Crumblin Alley, a clock struck one. "There's our man," whispered Dr. Bodgitt pointing to number four.

"We'll adopt the Lobster Squat," he added mysteriously. "It's an old espionage trick – works every time."

Without bothering to explain, Dr. Bodgitt slunk off in pursuit of Agent Ambel. Lucy and Jack followed stealthily.

They shadowed the man, dodging from doorway to doorway, as he wound through dark alleys and deserted passageways.

Suddenly Ambel broke into a run. Emerging into a wide street, he darted beneath an old rail bridge.

Lucy, Jack and Dr. Bodgitt raced after him at top speed. They were just in time to see him disappear into a metro station. They charged down the steps. Dr. Bodgitt was first to the ticket barrier. He rushed through, flourishing a special pass.

They burst on to the platform, just as the agent slipped aboard a train. Jack raced to the doors, but he was too late.

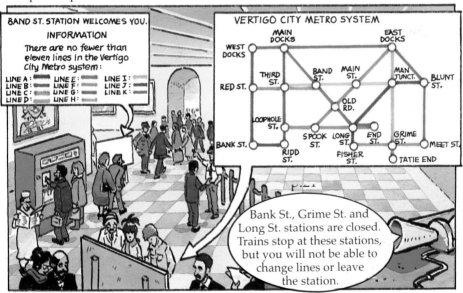

BAND ST. STATION WELCOMES YOU.

INFORMATION

There are no fewer than eleven lines in the Vertigo City Metro system:

LINE A: LINE E: LINE I:
LINE B: LINE F: LINE J:
LINE C: LINE G: LINE K:
LINE D: LINE H:

VERTIGO CITY METRO SYSTEM

WEST DOCKS • MAIN DOCKS • EAST DOCKS
THIRD ST. • BAND ST. • MAIN ST. • MAN JUNCT. • BLUNT ST.
RED ST.
OLD RD.
LOOPHOLE ST.
BANK ST. • SPOOK ST. • LONG ST. • END ST. • GRIME ST. • MEET ST.
RIDD ST. • FISHER ST. • TATIE END

Bank St., Grime St. and Long St. stations are closed. Trains stop at these stations, but you will not be able to change lines or leave the station.

"We'll never catch him now," groaned Lucy as they returned to the ticket hall.

But then she remembered the letter to "Mr. Raincoat."

With the help of the letter and a map of the metro system, they could discover exactly where the man was heading.

Where is Agent Ambel going?

To the Warehouse

They had to reach Loophole Street Station before Agent Ambel. "Let's take a taxi," cried Dr. Bodgitt, rushing back onto the street. Soon they were hurtling through the town.

They screeched to a halt at the station just as the agent dived into a warehouse. A few minutes later he appeared at an open window.

Dr. Bodgitt pointed to a fire escape on the other side of the street.

"From up there we should be able to see what Agent Ambel's doing," he said.

They laughed when I invented these giant collapsible binoculars, but they fit under a labcoat without leaving a bulge.

After a climb, Dr. Bodgitt scanned the warehouse through a pair of giant binoculars.

"I have the agent in my sights," muttered the doctor. "He seems to be hiding his briefcase."

Dr. Bodgitt whipped out a camera. "I must know what's in that briefcase," he cried. "We can photograph the contents."

"But first we have to get inside the place, and it's crawling with enemy agents," said Jack.

"Well, I could climb up the outside of the building," Lucy volunteered. Dr. Bodgitt handed her the special camera and she started to plan her route to the room where the briefcase was.

Can you see a safe route?

Behind Enemy Lines

After a perilous climb, Lucy swung down to the room. Perching on the ledge outside, she listened intently. Not a sound came from within and, judging it to be safe, Lucy slipped inside. She began a quick search for any information.

The floor was littered with pamphlets advertising something called the Ugleenian Dance Festival, but they weren't likely to help. Lucy opened a cabinet but it just contained more pamphlets. At that moment she heard footsteps . . .

. . . She dashed to the loose floorboard that Dr. Bodgitt had told her about, and pulled out the briefcase.

Inside were two pieces of paper. Snap! She photographed the papers, shoved the briefcase back in position . . .

. . . and leaped to the window. As she swung herself up the rope, she heard the agents burst into the room behind her.

Back on the ground, she hurried to Jack and Dr. Bodgitt. The doctor produced a strange looking device from his pocket.

"This is my portable film processor. All we need is a dark place," he explained, diving into a deserted cellar.

I've been having a few problems with the camera. Somehow the pictures seem to get jumbled up . . .

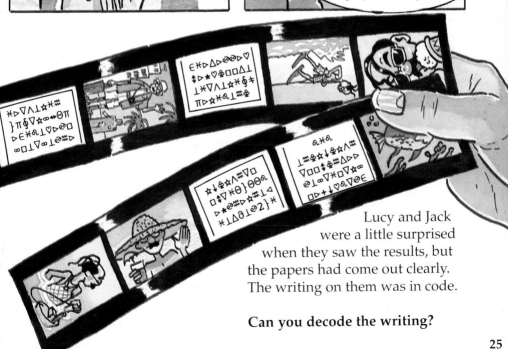

Lucy and Jack were a little surprised when they saw the results, but the papers had come out clearly. The writing on them was in code.

Can you decode the writing?

Landlock Wharf

With the help of Lucy's map, they soon found their way to Landlock Wharf and located the *Sinking Sally*.

"Luckily I have one of my newly developed bugging devices with me," whispered Dr. Bodgitt. "We'll just clamp it to the boat then listen to the rogues conspiring."

Unfortunately, two tough looking guards lounged on the towpath, watching the barge. Lucy spotted a rowing boat. They could borrow the boat and approach the barge from the water.

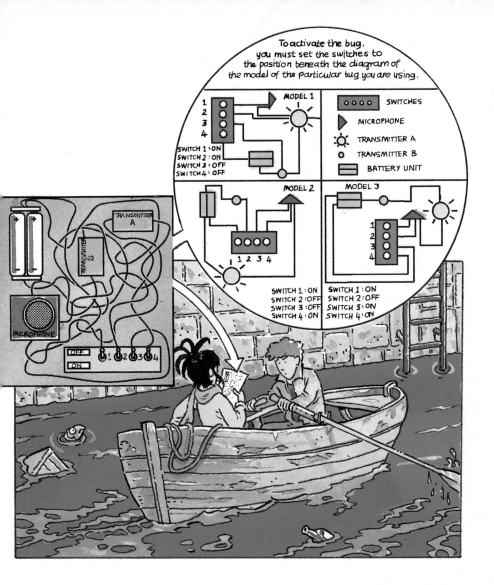

"You two go ahead," said Dr. Bodgitt. "All you have to do is activate the bug, then attach it to the barge. I'll - er- keep watch. I'm staying off boats since my experience on the *Esmerelda*."

Soon Lucy and Jack were rowing out onto the murky canal.

But as they drew alongside the *Sinking Sally*, they realized that Dr. Bodgitt had forgotten to tell them how to activate the bug. Lucy found some confusing instructions. Her first task was to find which kind of bug they had.

How can Lucy activate the bug?

Double Agent Lucy

Seconds later, Lucy snapped the bugging device into position.

"Mission accomplished," she hissed to Jack.

They returned to Dr. Bodgitt, who was frantically pressing buttons on his miniature receiver.

"It works!" he beamed, sounding a little surprised.

They listened to the voices crackling over the airwaves:

"Agent 598 will join us. We'll leave the moment she arrives. She'll be wearing a scarf and will give the passwords: 'It's cold in Uglee for the time of year' . . . She's still not here."

Lucy leaped to her feet, a plan forming in her mind. Before the others could stop her, she was dashing along the quayside to the *Sinking Sally*.

"I'm agent 598," she announced, jumping aboard. "It's ugly in cold for the time of year. I mean . . ."

The man scowled.

"You're a little young to be an agent," he said suspiciously, as the barge moved out onto the canal.

"It's a disguise," replied Lucy.

As the *Sinking Sally* nosed its way into a dark tunnel, the agent cut the engines.

To Lucy's amazement they drew alongside a massive steel door set into the tunnel wall. The agent punched a sequence into the electronic lock.

"This way," he growled as the doors slid noiselessly open.

D5 0500 AT C1 ENSURE THAT D6 THE LATEST B4 GIVE US C2 THE SCIENTISTS B1 THE INVISIBLE D4 HEADQUARTERS BY B5 THE FINAL C3 ARE READY A2 GAME IS D3 TO COMMAND B2 SPY IS A1 OPERATION POWER C4 TO PREPARE B7 THE XYL-O-PHONE D2 TO RETURN B8 280 FORMULA A3 NEARING COMPLETION C5 THE SUBSTANCE B3 ABOUT TO B6 PART OF D1 ALL AGENTS

Lucy stepped into a hi-tech laboratory. One of the enemy agents from the boat rushed over to a machine that was whirring and printing. He started reading the printout into a radio transmitter. At first, Lucy couldn't make sense of the jumbled words, but looking at the piece of paper, she realized she could piece together the message.

What does it say?

The Game is up

Lucy was horrified. The World Leaders of Tomorrow had the last part of the Xyl-o-phone 280 formula. The Invisible Spy had succeeded in his, or her, task!

The machine whirred into life again, and Lucy stared at the printout.

She had to warn Dr. Bodgitt. As one of the agents grabbed the formula and snapped it into a special cannister, Lucy sneaked through a doorway on the other side of the laboratory. She pulled out her Megatuff Radio, but the battery had fallen out!

Creeping up a small metal staircase, she found herself in a room filled with radio equipment. Perhaps she could contact Dr. Bodgitt. Suddenly the doors shut behind her, and the room began to move. She was inside some kind of communications truck!

Frantically, Lucy tried to operate the transmitters, without success. Then she tried the doors, but they were locked. The truck hurtled on through the night, then screeched to a halt.

When the doors opened, Lucy found herself at an old iron bridge, face to face with five sinister looking agents.

In an instant, she knew that her game was up.

Prisoner

Lucy made a sudden dash for freedom, but she was surrounded. In seconds she was in the clutches of the enemy agents.

Struggling desperately, she was dragged toward a motor launch.

As the launch sped out to sea, Lucy caught sight of a ship looming up out of the mist.

"Take her aboard the *Tretcheros*," snarled one of the agents. "Then we'll find out what she knows."

Put the cannister with the formula in cabin X17. We'll take it to the Spymaster's Headquarters as soon as the scientists are ready.

In minutes they were aboard the ship. Lucy was bundled into a stifling cabin next to the boiler room. With the door slammed shut, she searched for a way out.

Lucy caught sight of an open hatchway high on one wall. She began to climb.

She struggled through the narrow opening, then found herself sliding helter-skelter down a steep chute. Cautiously, Lucy climbed through another hatchway.

To her amazement, she found herself staring straight at a plan of the ship. Now she could find the way to the cabin where the agents had taken the formula.

What is Lucy's route?

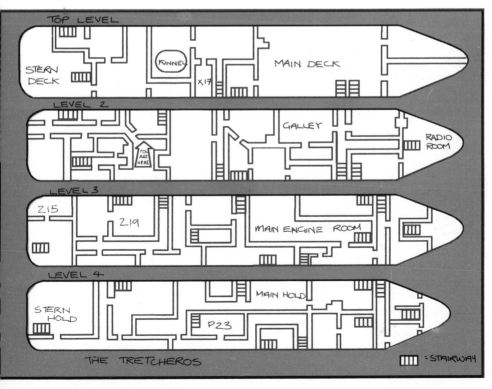

TOP LEVEL

STERN DECK

FUNNEL

X17

MAIN DECK

LEVEL 2

GALLEY

YOU ARE HERE

RADIO ROOM

LEVEL 3

215

219

MAIN ENGINE ROOM

LEVEL 4

STERN HOLD

P23

MAIN HOLD

THE TRETCHEROS

= STAIRWAY

Aboard the *Tretcheros*

> I can't see anyone

Lucy knew how to reach cabin X17, but at any moment she might bump into a villainous agent. She crept forward cautiously, but skidded on a patch of oil, and fell to the deck with a crash!

As two guards rushed to see what had caused the noise, Lucy flung herself behind a packing case. Trembling, she watched as the guards searched the deck. At last they retreated, muttering to each other.

A minute later, Lucy arrived at cabin X17. She crept inside, and began a swift search. The cannister containing the last part of the formula was nowhere to be found. The World Leaders of Tomorrow must have taken it to their headquarters already.

Lucy slumped down defeated. Then she spotted a bundle of papers. With the help of a chart and some complex instructions, she could locate the headquarters itself.

Where is it?

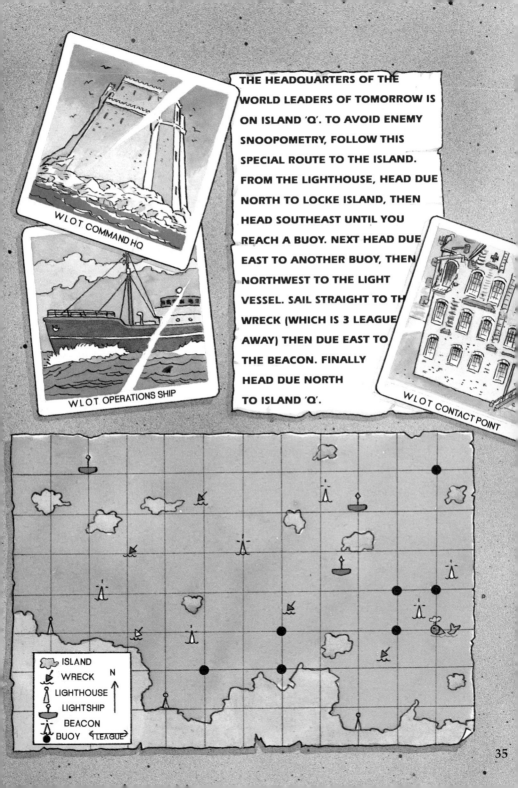

WLOT COMMAND HQ

WLOT OPERATIONS SHIP

WLOT CONTACT POINT

THE HEADQUARTERS OF THE WORLD LEADERS OF TOMORROW IS ON ISLAND 'Q'. TO AVOID ENEMY SNOOPOMETRY, FOLLOW THIS SPECIAL ROUTE TO THE ISLAND. FROM THE LIGHTHOUSE, HEAD DUE NORTH TO LOCKE ISLAND, THEN HEAD SOUTHEAST UNTIL YOU REACH A BUOY. NEXT HEAD DUE EAST TO ANOTHER BUOY, THEN NORTHWEST TO THE LIGHT VESSEL. SAIL STRAIGHT TO THE WRECK (WHICH IS 3 LEAGUES AWAY) THEN DUE EAST TO THE BEACON. FINALLY HEAD DUE NORTH TO ISLAND 'Q'.

ISLAND
WRECK
LIGHTHOUSE
LIGHTSHIP
BEACON
BUOY
LEAGUE
N

35

Island Fortress

Lucy had to contact Dr. Bodgitt and Jack. Spotting a transistor radio, Lucy took out the battery and slipped it into her Megatuff walkie-talkie. Quickly, she gabbled instructions.

Minutes later, Jack and Dr. Bodgitt drew alongside the *Tretcheros* in a speed boat. They sped through the choppy waters to the gang's headquarters, an old fortress built on an island.

I've put all my fellow agents on red alert. Once I press the button on my Micro-Tuned Homing Beacon, they'll be with us in seconds. But first we must unmask The Invisible Spy.

At last the enemy's headquarters towered above them.

Under cover of mist and darkness, they scaled the walls.

Lucy and Jack hauled Dr. Bodgitt into the fortress.

Once they were inside, Jack spotted a heavy door. At the same moment, they heard footsteps, and hid. They watched as an agent pressed various buttons on an electronic doorlock. Each of them memorised the part of the sequence that they had seen.

Can you unlock the door ?

The last button is bottom left . . .

Altogether six buttons were used.

The first button is top right . . . the next one is top left . . .

Attack!

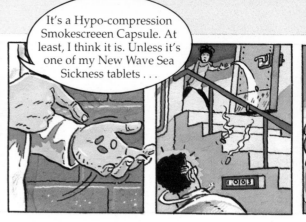

As the door swung open, the intrepid three slipped into a hallway. Dr. Bodgitt handed Lucy a small capsule, whispering an explanation.

Lucy crept down a flight of steps and spotted a door marked "Control Room". She hurled the capsule into the room . . . but would it work?

ED HARDFAH OF THE HARDFAH NEWS AGENCY. THIS MAN IS AN ALLY OF DR BODGITT. HE HAS BEEN WORKING AS AN UNDER-COVER AGENT FOR FIFTEEN YEARS. HE MUST BE ELIMINATED.

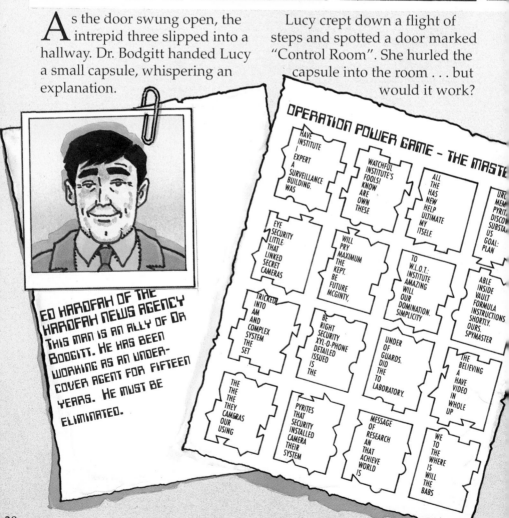

Instantly dense smoke billowed out. Enemy agents ran choking and spluttering in every direction.

"Eureka!" cried Dr. Bodgitt.

As they raced into the control room, Lucy almost tripped over a low table littered with papers.

"Look at these!" she gasped.

"Lucy" – an ally of Dr. Bodgitt

DATE	LOCAL TIDE CHART	
	HIGH TIDE	LOW TIDE
September 22	21:31	09:34
September 23	21:48	09:42
September 24	22:06	10:03
September 25	22:19	10:11

CONTROL ROOM

89H   RB11

STORE ROOM

748

One of the papers was headed: "Operation Power Game – The Masterplan". The rest of the writing was in code, but Lucy was sure this document held the key to the whole mystery.

If they could decode it, perhaps they would at last be able to unmask "The Invisible Spy."

Can you decipher the writing?

The Spymaster at Last

N ow everything made sense. The Invisible Spy was a camera, planted at the Institute by the "security expert". No wonder no one had ever seen the spy!

The moment of triumph was short-lived. Accompanied by two burly henchmen, the Spymaster herself burst into the room. She snarled a grim order.

Just then Dr. Bodgitt's backup agents swarmed into the room.

Enemy agents grabbed their secret equipment and tried to escape.

Lucy spotted the Spymaster slipping through a doorway, and followed.

They ran back to the control room. "She's got the cannister with the formula," gasped Lucy.

"After her!" cried Dr. Bodgitt, heroically flinging himself at the fleeing figure . . . and missing. Babs McGinty laughed and reached her goal .

She dashed through a doorway in the control panel which then closed up behind her. There was nothing they could do.

But then Jack's face lit up. He knew that Babs's plan would fail.

What has Jack realized?

What the Papers Say

FLOWER POWER!

Scientists working at the world famous Pyrites Institute have invented an amazing new substance called Xyl-o-phone 281. Made from the petals of the common plant, "Purple Timpany", Xyl-o-phone 281 will be used to generate heat and light throughout the world, very cheaply and without any harmful side effects.

EARLIER VERSION

An earlier version of the substance, Xyl-o-phone 280, could have been used to make weapons. The formula for this substance has now been destroyed.

BODGITT IS NEW HEAD

Following the retirement of Professor Franklin Pipette, the Pyrites Institute has appointed Dr Bartholemew Bodgitt as its new head.

Dr. Bodgitt is pictured here with his latest creation, The Wonder Wig. "It grows like real hair," claims the doctor.

WORLD LEADERS OF YESTERDAY

At the end of a sensational trial, members of a sinister group calling themselves the "World Leaders of Tomorrow"(W.L.O.T.) have been found guilty of "conspiring to take over the entire world by force". All seventeen members of W.L.O.T., including their leader Babs McGinty, were caught in a daring dawn raid at an offshore fortress.

Members of another gang, led by Johnny "Green" Raincoat, were found guilty of kidnapping, theft and holding loud parties after 11pm.

Babs McGinty - "A devious and dastardly criminal".

JUNIOR REPORTER WINS TOP AWARD

Junior reporter Lucy Lambert has scooped the coveted Gnu News Award for a gripping account of her part in bringing the "World Leaders of Tomorrow" to justice. Lucy, who works for the Hardfax News Agency, says she is thrilled by the award. However, Lucy is not sure if she'll stay in journalism. She is tempted by the danger and excitement of life as a secret agent ...

Lucy Lambert receives her award from the newly-appointed Cultural Attaché of Uglee, Her Marvelousness Agnes Glulck.

SMOKE MYSTERY EXPLAINED

In an exclusive interview, Doctor Bartholemew Bodgitt of the Pyrites Research Institute has revealed that he was behind the mysterious smoke that filled Trankwill Square last Tuesday. "I was fleeing a band of ruthless kidnappers," explains Bodgitt. Trapped inside the Pyrites Laboratory, Dr Bodgitt hurled a special Smokescreen capsule into the square below. "Then," says Bodgitt, I removed the bars from an upstairs window and climbed down a rope, hoping to slip away unnoticed." But did the ingenious escape bid work? Says Bodgitt: "In the confusion, unfortunately I - er bumped straight into my kidnappers."

Clues

Answers

Pages 2-3

Lucy must greet Dr. Bodgitt as "Your Marvelousness". She should expect him to reply "Your Greatness".

She knows this because Dr. Bodgitt tells her to use the titles of the Ambassador of Uglee and his wife and two of the pieces of paper on the notice board tell her what these titles are.

Pages 4-5

The meeting point, below the One-Eared Zebek, is shown here.

Pages 6-7

The letter has been written back to front, with the sign / between words. To decipher the message, Lucy and Jack start at the bottom right hand corner of the page and read each word backwards, adding punctuation. This is what the letter says:

I am in terrible danger. Enemy agents are after me. I will try to get to one of the safe houses but I do not know if I will succeed. In this envelope you will find some negatives and a coded message dropped by a spy ring agent. I have translated the message, which is in Cipher Baloney Three. I hope it helps. I also overheard Green Raincoat planning a meeting in Kard Alley at seven-thirty tonight. Perhaps you should go there and arrest him and his cronies. Bodgitt.

Pages 8-9

The photo shows Dr. Bodgitt being dragged into Number 12, Block Street by two men.

Pages 10-11

Lucy puts together the message by taking the first letter of each word in the ad. This then reads:

BODGITT JETTY NUMBER TWENTY

Pages 12-13

The boat the kidnappers are using is the *Esmerelda*. Lucy and Jack know this because of the translated note they found with Dr. Bodgitt's letter. It explained that "the prisoner" would be taken to "*Esmerelda*" for questioning.

Pages 14-15

We know that the second button is seven below the first. Therefore the second button must be in one of the bottom two rows, and the first must be in one of the top two rows. Since the third button is in the same row as the second, its symbol must be either a triangle or a star. The fourth button is five above the fifth, so it must be in one of the top four rows. As there are no star symbols in the top four rows, the fourth button (and therefore the first and the third, which both have the same symbol) is definitely labelled with a triangle. There is only one triangle in the top two rows, and this must therefore be the first button. Once you have found the first button, you can work out where the other ones are. It's easier than it sounds!

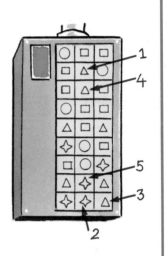

Pages 18-19

Dr. Bodgitt's decoder replaces every vowel with a symbol. A prints out as ϒ, E as φ, I as ψ, O as Σ and U as ϑ. Once punctuation has been added, the message should read:

Dear Mr. Raincoat,

When we handed over Dr. Bodgitt to the World Leaders of Tomorrow, I discovered some information that might be useful. One of the World Leaders, who is called Agent Ambel, will leave 4 Umbrella Alley at one o' clock tomorrow morning. If he uses the metro he will go two stops exactly, then change lines, then he will go one stop and change lines again. After that he will go one stop, then change, then three stops, then change, then one stop, and leave the station. Also, the Spymaster has a special bunker where she keeps a submarine, but the bunker can only be used at high tide. Access is from a secret door in the control room at World Leaders' HQ. This door leads only to the bunker. I hope this information is useful, sir.

Red Scarf.

Pages 20-21

Agent Ambel starts at Band Street. Following his instructions he then goes two stops to Man Junction, one stop to Blunt Street, then one stop to East Docks. After that he goes three stops to Spook Street and finally one stop to Loophole Street. This is his destination.

Pages 22-23

Lucy's route to the room with the briefcase is shown in red.

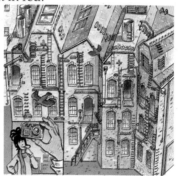

Pages 24-25

You can find out which symbol stands for which letter in this code by using Dr. Bodgitt's translation of the note on page 7. Then it is easy to decipher the words on the papers, revealing the following message:

To agents 485 and 108 of the World Leaders of Tomorrow: You will meet agent 598 on the Sinking Sally at 0400 hours on September 24th. The Sinking Sally is moored at Landlock Wharf.

Pages 26-27

The only circuit diagram that matches the bug that Lucy and Jack have is Model 3. To activate their bug they must set:

Switch 1: on
Switch 2: off
Switch 3: on
Switch 4: off

Pages 28-29

This message isn't strictly in code. It's just that the sentences have been jumbled up. Lucy notices that in front of each pair of words there is a letter and a number. She realizes that each letter stands for a sentence, and each number shows the position of the words in the sentence. By arranging each pair of words in the order A1, A2, A3 , B1 and so on, she reads:

Operation Power Game is nearing completion. The Invisible Spy is about to give us the final part of the Xyl-o-phone 280 formula. Ensure that the scientists are ready to prepare the substance. All agents to return to command headquarters by 0500 at the latest.

Pages 32-33

The route Lucy takes to cabin X17 of the *Tretcheros* is shown in red.

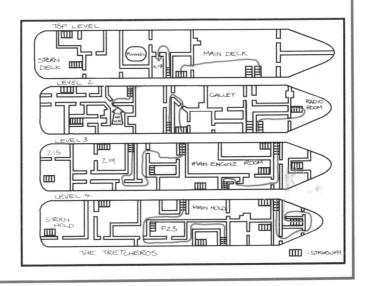

Pages 34-35

Island Q is circled in black. The lighthouse you have to start from must be this one.

If you follow the instructions from either of the others, you will not come across all the landmarks that are mentioned.

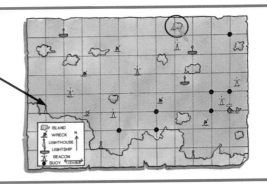

Pages 36-37

The cross on each button in the sequence has been rotated 45 degrees clockwise from its position on the previous button. The symbols have also been moved around but they remain in the same order. The correct sequence is shown here.

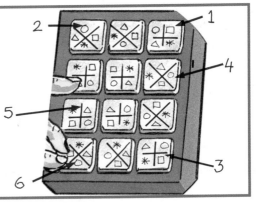

Pages 38-39

In fact, the Masterplan is not written in code, but has been cut up rather like a jigsaw. Fit the pieces together, and you will find out who The Invisible Spy is. The complete Masterplan reads:

Urgent message to all members of W.L.O.T. The Pyrites Research Institute has discovered an amazing new substance that will help us achieve our ultimate goal: world domination. My plan is simplicity itself. I have tricked the Pyrites Institute into believing that I am a security expert and have installed a complex video camera surveillance system in their building. The whole system was set up under the watchful eye of the institute's security guards. The fools! Little did they know that the cameras are linked to our own secret laboratory. Using these cameras we will be able to pry right inside the maximum security vault where the Xyl-o-phone formula is kept. Detailed instructions will be issued shortly. The future is ours!

Babs McGinty, The Spymaster.

Pages 40-41

Hoping to flee by submarine, Babs McGinty has disappeared into her secret bunker. But Jack has realized that she is not as devious as she thinks . . .

In his letter on page 19, Red Scarf explained that the submarine can only be used at high tide which, according to the chart on page 39, is at 22:06 on that day (September 24th). We know the date from the message on page 25.

The clock in the control room shows that the time is only 10:03, which means that the tide is at its lowest. The Spymaster is therefore trapped in the bunker.

First published in 1993 by Usborne Publishing Ltd, Usborne House, 83-85 Saffron Hill, London EC1N 8RT, England. Copyright © 1993 Usborne Publishing Ltd.

The name Usborne and the device are Trade Marks of Usborne Publishing Ltd. All rights reserved.